For Tola, Temi, Teja, and all the real-life Selahs who inspired this story.
Continue shining brighter than a thousand suns.—TA

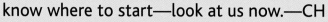

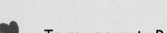 To my parents Perry and Darnie and my siblings Bruiser, Ciji, and Char—I love you all
so much. To my Uncle Ivey, who continues to cheer for me from his place in the sky—I
miss you. You believed in me every step of the way and encouraged me through times of
doubt. We all miss you and your jokes. To this day, I still say no one can make red velvet
cake quite like you can. And to the young girl who wanted to be an artist, but didn't
know where to start—look at us now.—CH

Library of Congress Control Number: 2023932930
ISBN 9781959244028

Text copyright © 2023 by Tonya Abari
Illustrations by Chasity Hampton
Illustrations copyright © 2023 Chasity Hampton

Published by The Innovation Press
7511 Greenwood Avenue N. #4132, Seattle, WA 98103
www.theinnovationpress.com

Printed and bound by Worzalla
Production date June 2023

Cover art by Chasity Hampton
Book layout by Tim Martyn

LOCS

NOT
DREADS

WRITTEN BY TONYA ABARI   ILLUSTRATED BY CHASITY HAMPTON

One crisp fall morning, Selah was feelin' herself.
Glisten!
Her slide was electric as she danced down the driveway.

On the way to the bus stop, Selah pulled her thick, ropelike locs into a high ponytail and smiled.

She couldn't wait to get to school and show off her newly loc'd hair!

Phhhsssttt!
The big yellow bus pulled up to the front of the
school, and Selah quickly hopped off.

But she slowed down when a handful of students began whispering and pointing at her hair.

"Hey everybody, look at Selah's dreadlocks!" a classmate yelled.

She'd never heard her family use the word dreadlocks before.
And when Selah heard the word dread, it made her think of
many hair-raising things.

Suddenly, Selah's scary thoughts were interrupted by Principal Carver's arm on her shoulders.

"Words are powerful, Selah. But there's absolutely nothing dreadful about your hair."

Still, Selah felt uneasy.
Too many eyes were on her locs.

In class.

At recess.

And even Selah's best friend, Britt, couldn't stop staring at her locs during lunch.

That afternoon, Selah wasn't feelin' herself.
Her legs were heavy as she climbed the hill home.

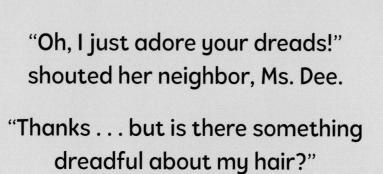

"Oh, I just adore your dreads!"
shouted her neighbor, Ms. Dee.

"Thanks . . . but is there something
dreadful about my hair?"

"No, baby. Your hair is big,
bold, and beautiful!" said Ms. Dee.

Selah appreciated Ms. Dee's
praise, but she wondered again,
"Is there something scary
about my locs?"

Selah made her way through the front door and into the kitchen. Nana Pearl was retightening Daddy's locs with coconut oil and berry pomade. It smelled like tropical trees and candy.

Straight fiyah!

"Pull up a chair, Selah," Daddy said. "We were just reminiscing about your brother's locs when he was your age."

"Jeremy's hair was so full and long, it couldn't even fit under the largest baseball helmet," Mama added. "Coach sent a letter home asking us to shave off Jeremy's locs."

TO THE PARENT/GUARDIAN OF JEREMY DAVIS:

I hope this letter finds you well! Jeremy is such a valuable addition to our baseball team. However, I discovered during practice that his dreadlocks don't fit beneath the batting helmet. Safety is our top priority. We can't risk Jeremy's hair getting tangled with other objects on the field or having his helmet fall off at the mound.

I am also concerned that his hair might be a distraction because there aren't any other players with dreadlocks. If Jeremy wants to continue playing baseball, I highly suggest cutting Jeremy's dreadlocks. Please feel free to drop by or give me a call if you have any questions.

Sincerely,

Selah thought about Ms. Dee . . . and the
comments and stares at school.

"Is there something terrifying about our locs?"
she asked.

"Of course not," Jeremy responded. "Our locs are amazing. Our locs are delightful. Our locs are magical."

"Then why would people use a word like dread to describe our hair?" asked Selah.

"Well, there are many stories behind the origins of loc'd hair," explained Mama.

"That's right," echoed Nana. "Locs have been worn throughout history. But some say that long ago, warriors loc'd their hair to put terror into the hearts of their enemies. Others say that dreadlocks was a term used by people who were afraid because they never saw locs before. And some, who even called themselves Dreads, believed that wearing locs reflected a deep respect for the Almighty."

"And that's why we wear locs with pride," Daddy said.
"The strength of our ancestors lives in each strand.
No matter what anyone calls them—locs, dreadlocks, or dreads—
our hair is liberation."

Selah looked at her family and paused.

"Well, did you do it, Mama . . .
did you shave off
Jeremy's locs?"

"Absolutely not!" Jeremy jumped in. "We pinned them down under my helmet, and I was back in the batter's box in no time."

Now, it was all starting to make sense.
"Locs aren't dreadful at all!"

Selah couldn't wait to go back to school and floss her beautifully loc'd hair.

The next morning, Selah was feelin' herself.
Flawless!
She pranced through the front door with a pep in her step and marched down the driveway, spirit soaring above the clouds.

On the way to the bus stop, Selah made sure her new, sparkly charms were in place.

Phhhsssttt!
The big yellow bus pulled up
to the front of the school,
and Selah jumped off.

Britt approached Selah and
tapped her on the shoulder.

"Hi, Selah . . . I wanted to tell you yesterday
that I really love your dr—"

"Locs." Selah raised her head high.
"You really love my *locs.*"

Britt smiled. "Yes, I really love your locs."

Selah was definitely feelin' herself now. "They *are* pretty fierce, aren't they?"

Dear fabulous reader,

Thank you for going on this journey with me! Selah's story was inspired by my eight-year-old niece's locs. What started as a way to maintain healthy hair and celebrate our history became an opportunity to learn about the beauty and origins of loc'd hair. Reading about the history of loc'd hair, seeing magnificent loc'd styles, and thinking deeply about word choice helped to promote self-love, even in the face of hair discrimination.

This is an important and ongoing conversation. If you are a reader with locs, I see you. I support you. I believe in you. As you continue to shine, repeat these affirmative phrases into a mirror: I am worthy of praise. I matter. I am beautiful. I am surrounded by people who are rooting for me. I love everything about my locs. I love everything about myself!

I hope you will join me for many more adventures, readers. Until next time . . .

Peace, love, and locs,

Sonya Abasi

FREQUENTLY ASKED QUESTIONS

What are the different ways someone can wear their locs?

Locs are a universal hairstyle that can be worn for many reasons. Whether they are worn for spiritual, cultural, religious, or ethnic reasons, or just as a fashion statement, locs are very versatile! There are sisterlocks, faux locs, freeform, and goddess locs. They can be worn up or down, with jewelry or without, ponytailed, with a pop of color, messy bunned, or pulled into a French braid. What's your favorite loc'd style?

How are locs formed?

Locs begin with coils, palm rolls, backcombing, free forming, interlocking, sponging, two-strand twists, or mini braids – and then they just grow, grow, grow, and grow some more! I know how to start and maintain our locs, but you can also see a stylist, called a loctician, who specializes in loc'd hair.

How exactly did you install your locs, Nana?

Well, I have crochet locs. That means I attached already loc'd hair to my own loose, natural hair. I started with about ten cornrows against my scalp and added hair using a crochet hook and interlocking method.

Is caring for locs any different than caring for other types of hair?

Depending on the specific style, loc'd hair might require a few unique products for styling, but generally good hair care means keeping locs clean and moisturized. It's best to research your own hair type and figure out which routine works best for you!

I heard someone use the word "unprofessional" when referring to loc'd hair. Are locs okay to wear to school and work?

Of course they are! Locs are professional because hair does not determine how well you can perform at work or school. There has been a long history of hair discrimination in places like work and school. However, there are now laws being passed to ensure people with natural styles like locs are treated equally at school and at work.

A CELEBRATION OF LOCS